PIPPBROOK BOOKS

First published in the UK in 1999 by Templar Publishing
This softback edition produced in 2013 by Pippbrook Books,
an imprint of The Templar Company Limited,
Deepdene Lodge, Deepdene Avenue, Dorking, Surrey, RH5 4AT, UK
www.templarco.co.uk

ISBN 978-1-84877-764-4

Designed by Hayley Bebb and Manhar Chauhan
Edited by Dugald Steer and Liza Miller

Printed in Singapore

Elisa

The *The* BUNNY of
BLUEBELL HILL

WRITTEN BY TIM PRESTON   ILLUSTRATIONS BY LORNA HUSSEY

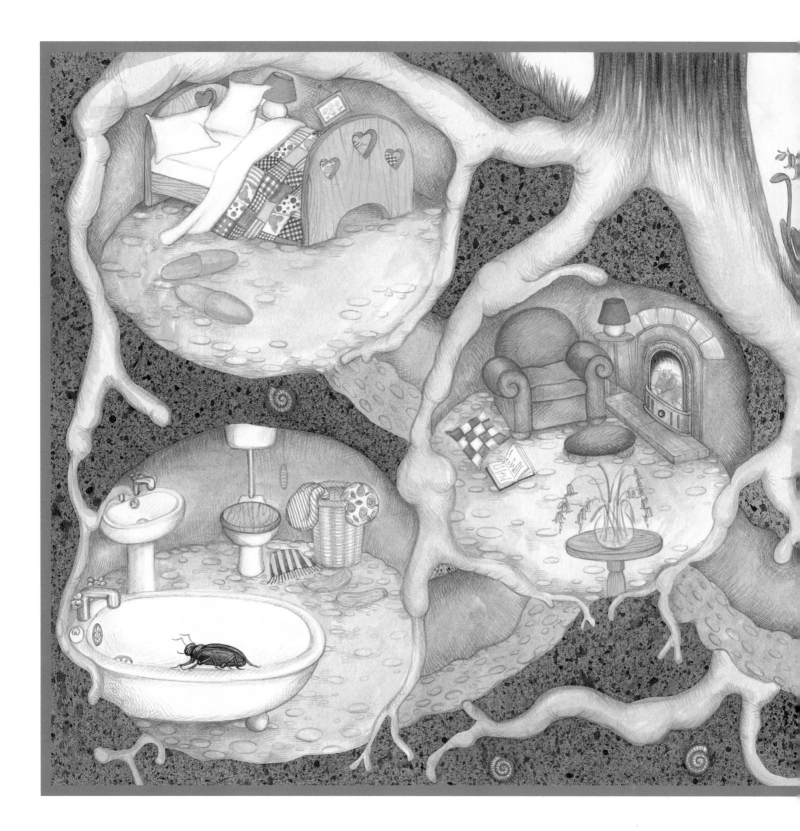

At the top of Bluebell Hill
there was an old oak tree. And underneath
that oak tree there was a burrow,
and in that burrow lived a bunny.
It was a very nice burrow, with four little rooms
and bluebells growing by the front door.

But Bunny didn't like it.

"I am bored with this burrow,"
said Bunny to herself.
"I am tired of walking up and down this hill.
I am fed up with being hit on the head by acorns.
And I am very, very bored with bluebells!

I want an exciting new home."

So without further ado, she
set off to find herself one.

Bunny's friend Squirrel took her to see
his high-rise tree-house. But Bunny
didn't have a head for heights!
And her big paws just weren't meant for jumping
about from branch to branch.

"I'm sorry, Squirrel," said Bunny.
"I think I need something a little closer to the ground!"

The next animal Bunny visited was Badger.
He lived in a mossy bank in the heart of the
old forest. It was dark and still among the trees,
and there weren't many passers-by,
which was just the way
Badger liked it.

"But it's too quiet for me!" said Bunny.

"If you like company, why not try
living by the river?" suggested Otter.
"There's always lots going on down here."
But Bunny only had to take one look at Otter's
houseboat to know that it wouldn't suit her.

"It's much too wet here for me!" she wailed.

"Hmmm, then what about the meadow where
Field Mouse lives?" suggested Otter.

Field Mouse seemed happy living in the meadow,
but no matter how hard she tried, Bunny
just could not get comfortable there.

For a start there was no shade anywhere
and when the sun beat down it was very hot!

And the pollen from the poppies was extremely
sneezy, and the corn-stalks were scratchy.

So that was no good either.

"What about Owl's house?" suggested Field Mouse.
Owl lived in the loft of the old barn.
It was certainly dry, and very clean,
but there was something wrong with it too.
"It's just too draughty," said Bunny.

Would she ever find

a new home?

By the mountain the little rabbit found an
empty cave. It was slightly gloomy, but at least there was
lots of space. She thought it might be just the place,
until she heard a grumbly, growly sort of sound.
Then she realised — it was Bear's house!

"And Bear snores too much," said Bunny.

"I couldn't possibly live near him!"

The cave

Bunny was about to give up when she found
a smart blue door in the roots of a chestnut tree.
"This would be perfect!" said Bunny to herself.

But something seemed wrong.
The place had a funny smell —
a frightful, foxy sort of smell...

Suddenly, Bunny felt very afraid and she ran away,
as fast as she could.

Bunny ran and ran, past the barn and the field,
the river and the forest, all the way back to Bluebell Hill.
She ran up the hill, past the bluebells and straight in
through her own front door.

Bunny looked around her little burrow.
"It's not too hot or too wet. It's not too quiet or too noisy.
In fact, it's the perfect place for me!"

And so it was!